Stretchy
and Beanie

Judy Schachner

Dial Books for Young Readers

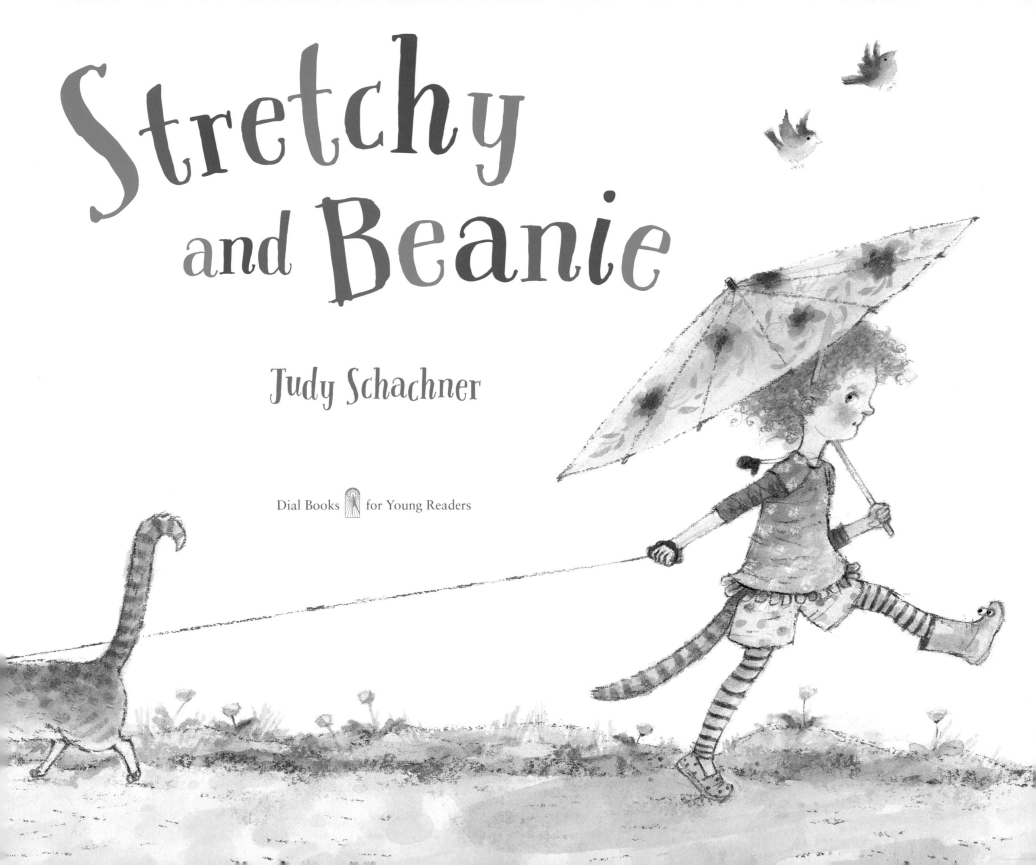

FOR DR. ANDREA LERNER AND HER
FELINE-LOVING STAFF AT JUST FOR CATS

Dial Books for Young Readers, An imprint of Penguin Random House LLC, New York

First published in the United States of America by Dial Books for Young Readers,
an imprint of Penguin Random House LLC, 2021

Dial & colophon are registered trademarks of Penguin Random House LLC.

Visit us online at penguinrandomhouse.com.

Library of Congress Cataloging-in-Publication Data is available.

Manufactured in China • ISBN 9780593111611 • 10 9 8 7 6 5 4 3 2 1

Design by Lily Malcom • Text set in Sabon

The art for this book was created in acrylics, gouache, collage, and mixed media.

Bonus Audio read by the author available here:
penguin.com/stretchyandbeanie *
*requires signup for news
from Penguin Random House

When the McHandsome Clan
met the McBrights,
each kid got a cat,
so it worked out just right.

Fergus friended Jordy,

McDoogle
circled Earl,

Callie and Joy tickled
Pickles and Pearl.

Roo ran to Tiny,

Jamie rolled
with Finny,

Cocoa cuddled Roy,

and Quentin
hugged Ol' Binny.

But when it came to Beanie,
Stretchy took the prize,
for they had much more in common
than the color of their eyes.

Call it intuition,
but she felt he was her twin.
Like some cosmic kitty fairy tale
that made them next of kin.

Both were wild and woolly,
the wildest ever seen.
Of all the fearsome tigers,
they were the king and queen.

At first their days were glorious.
All was going well.
They practiced carving stretchy marks
 until the dinner bell.

They did stretches every afternoon
on special spongy mats,

the Tippytoenas

the Purr Diver

the Martha Graham

each doing what the other did,
like proper copycats.

The Big Bahookie

The Cul-de-Sac

Then Beanie got the bright idea
to raise a perfect pet.
Even read a big best seller
on how she could, and yet . . .

It would take a lot of work, she knew,
but Beanie didn't care.
She'd already been a mother
to a troop of teddy bears.

Next day bright and early,
she started in with lessons—
Math, Music, Dance, and Art
in twenty-minute sessions.

Stretchy did not like his lessons,
did not want to dance.
He'd rather eat a cantaloupe
than wear those fancy pants.

Still Beanie was determined
to make her boy obey.

She put him in a harness
so Stretchy couldn't stray.

When the kitty wouldn't budge,

not even for
a treat . . .

Beanie got
the stroller out
and
rolled
him
down
the
street.

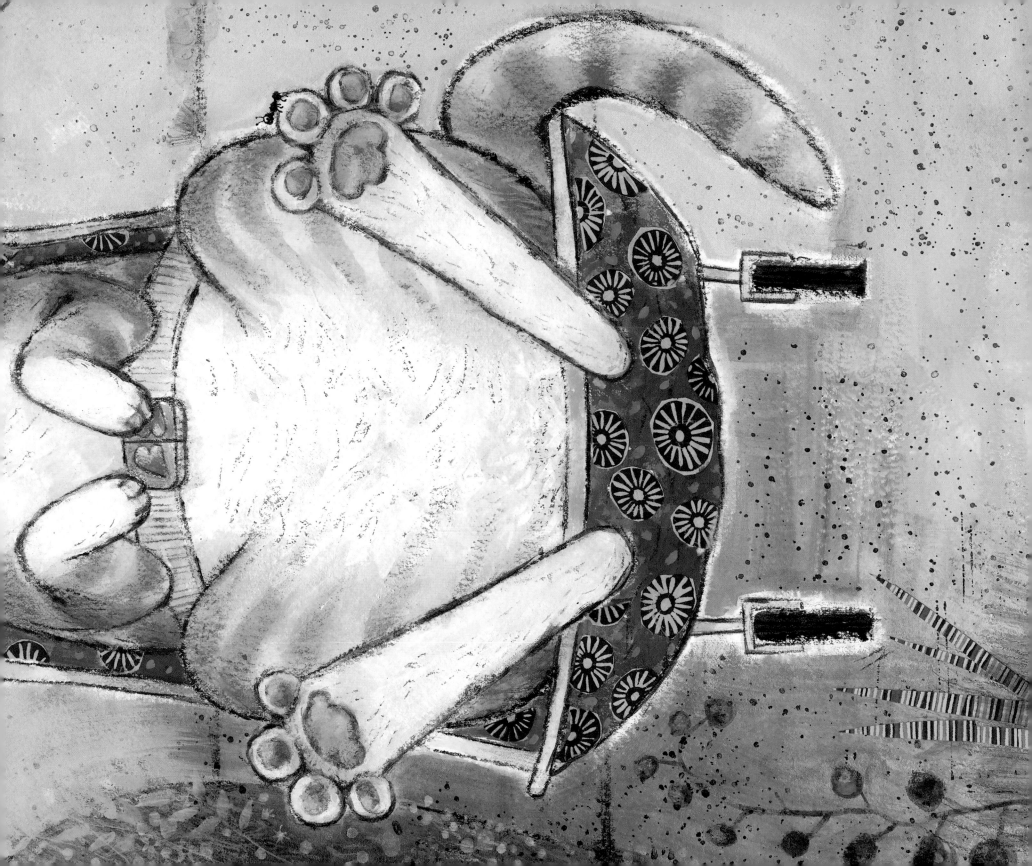

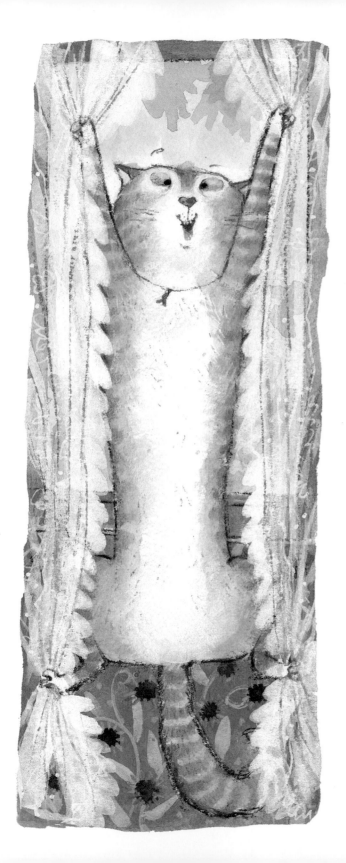

Stretchy wasn't ready
to be anyone's perfect pet.
He acted out, he climbed the drapes,
and made the carpet wet.

But what really curled his whiskers, aside from squeezy squishes,

was Beanie's firm belief in the benefit of kisses.

And though it wasn't possible
to love a kitty more,
was "Too Much Love" the reason
Stretchy howled at the door?

Or hid beneath a chair?
Or high up on a shelf

next to the cookies
and a strange little elf?

Strreeeeeeee

It wasn't love that got his goat.
'Twas all the other stuff.
Like learning to be perfect (huh!),
Stretchy'd had ENOUGH!

So it shouldn't be surprising
that he managed to get free.
Someone left the door ajar . . .

. . . and he scrambled up a tree.

Beanie was beside herself.
She had to get him back.
Especially since he thought of birds
as little flying snacks.

Yikes!

Stretchy climbed up higher.
He swung from limb to limb,
just like a ginger monkey
on a leafy jungle gym.

When finally he took a rest
stretched out upon a branch,

Beanie made a promise
to give him one more chance.

Puhleeeez!

But the lad refused to listen.
He proceeded to the top,
ignoring Beanie's orders
to STOP! STRETCHY! STOP!

Balancing above the world
while Beanie cried below,
Stretchy wondered what he'd do
with no place else to go.

Who would bring him dinner?
And brush his ginger fur?
And listen to him practice
his extraordinary purr?

The answer to these questions sat at the bottom of the tree,
surrounded by eight kitties and her bewildered family.

Then her brothers and her sisters
gave Beanie wise advice:
"If you want your kitty back,
don't be bossy, just be nice."

Now, I won't go into details
on how she got him down.

But it did involve two bags of snacks
and a fire truck from town.

It ended with apologies,
a smushy hug and kiss.
Of course Beanie overdid it,
which caused our lad to hiss.

But the lesson Beanie's learning
(though she hasn't learned it yet),
is PATIENCE, Love, and Kindness
make a perfect pet . . .

. . . or not.